Spoils of Success

by Larry Weinberg
illustrated by Tom Tierney

A GOLDEN BOOK ★ NEW YORK
Western Publishing Company, Inc., Racine, Wisconsin 53404

"I'm beat!" said Jerrica Benton as she and the Holograms came home after a long recording session. In her secret identity, she was Jem, the Holograms' leader.

"What's all that crying?" asked Aja. Some of the orphan girls who lived with them in Starlight Mansion were watching the news and sobbing.

"It's the earthquake in Zania," said Jerrica's sister, Kimber. "I wish we could help the people there."

"Maybe we can raise some money," said Jerrica.

"Hello!" called a voice. "Your front door was open."
The Holograms were amazed to see Eric Raymond.
Jerrica said, "We thought you were still in jail."
"No, I'm out on parole," said the former manager of
their rival group, the Misfits. "And since I once tried to
cheat you, I want to prove I've changed. Will you help me?
I'd like to star Jem and the Holograms in a concert to help
those earthquake victims. We'll raise millions. What do
you say?"

The Holograms looked at each other. They had to admit it was a terrific idea. "Except for one thing," said Shana. "With him, there's always an angle."

"OK," cried Raymond. "I'll level with you. I'm a jailbird. And the Misfits dumped me. But if I raise lots of money for those earthquake victims, I'll look good in the business again. Everybody wins!"

Jerrica sighed. "So what do we do, girls?"

"Let's go for it!" they answered.

Eric Raymond lost no time in moving into an office in Mammoth Stadium, where the concert was to be held.

"Hey, boss," said Zipper, his right-hand man. "Everybody is in for a big surprise when they see you working with the Holograms."

"They're in for another one when they hear how much I'm charging for a ticket. But it's for charity, right?" said Raymond. "Now, get out of my chair and watch the old master here zap out that publicity!"

A few days later, the Holograms were rehearsing in the stadium. Jerrica had transformed herself into Jem by using her earrings to call on the holographic powers of her computer, called Synergy.

Suddenly the Misfits barged in. Pizzazz was waving a copy of *Music Makers* magazine. "We just read about this gig," she said, "and we've got news for you. Raymond owes us all kinds of money. Our lawyers are going to stop this concert until we get paid."

"We might change our minds," she continued, "if *we're* in it, too—with top billing in everything!"

The Holograms went off to talk it over. "That's blackmail." "But what else can we do?" "Nothing. We're stuck."

Jem walked back to the Misfits. "All right," she said. "But this is pretty dirty."

"Oh, we know," said Pizzazz while Roxy and Stormer grinned. "That's why we like it so much."

A few days later, as the Holograms were out for a drive, Aja cried, "Look up there! 'Top billing in everything' is right!"

"You mean *total* billing!" said Kimber. "We're not mentioned on anything!"

"Listen to this," interrupted Shana, tuning in the car radio.

A reporter was saying, "Tell me, Pizzazz, who thought of this wonderful idea for a concert?"

"Oh…mostly me…and also Roxy and Stormer. Our manager, Eric Raymond, helped, too."

"Their manager!" cried Aja and Kimber together.

"It looks as if he was trying to win them back all along," said Jerrica. "*That* was his angle!"

If so, Eric Raymond was certainly doing a good job of publicizing the Misfits. The next week the mayor presented them with a gigantic key to the city.

And the week after that, the President of the United States shook hands with them before the cameras on the White House lawn.

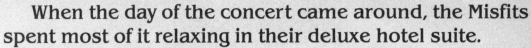

When the day of the concert came around, the Misfits spent most of it relaxing in their deluxe hotel suite.

"This article," said Roxy, looking up from a newspaper, "says our fans are starting to think we only pretend to be nasty and mean—that maybe we're really very nice."

"Isn't that great!" cried Stormer in delight.

"What do you mean 'great'?" screamed Pizzazz. "*Nice* ruins our whole image!" And without saying another word, she rushed out the door and left the hotel.

Hopping mad, Pizzazz took a taxi to Raymond's office in the stadium. He and Zipper were just leaving with huge sacks. They were stealing the ticket money!

"I'll split it with you," said Raymond calmly. "There's enough here for your own recording studio. You can put the Holograms in the shade every day of the week."

Pizzazz fell silent. Raymond's scheme was too wicked for her to go along with. She said, "That money goes to the people who were in the earthquake. All of it!"

"OK, OK," said Raymond. "I didn't mean to steal it in the beginning anyway. I just couldn't resist. Zipper, let's put this in the storeroom."

"Sure, boss," said Zipper, stepping up behind Pizzazz and pushing her into the tiny room. "That's exactly where *this* goes!" And he locked the door.

"We'd better get to that helicopter now," Pizzazz heard Raymond say. "Where did you hide it?"

"By the farm off River Road." And they ran off.

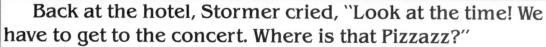

Back at the hotel, Stormer cried, "Look at the time! We have to get to the concert. Where is that Pizzazz?"

"Search me," said Roxy. "But she wouldn't miss a gig like this if she were dying."

"Well, I've called everyone I can think of."

"Most of her old pals don't have any phones. Come on, let's hit the streets."

The two Misfits searched every hangout they could think of, but not a soul among them had seen Pizzazz.

When evening came, the fans poured into the vast
stadium. By the thousands…the tens of thousands…
the hundreds of thousands they came. As they waited for
the concert to begin their excitement grew. And soon they
were shouting the names of their favorite groups.
    "HOLOGRAMS!"
    "MISFITS!"

As it grew late, Rio, the Holograms' manager—and Jerrica's boyfriend—knocked frantically on their dressing-room door.

"Listen," he told them. "I don't know what's happened to the Misfits. Or Eric Raymond." He looked around the room. "Oh, no! You've got to go on now—and I don't see Jem either!" Jerrica had never told him about her other identity.

"Not to worry," said Jerrica. "She's in the next room."

"Oh, Jem, dear!" she called as she started out the door. "You'd better hurry up."

The moment she was out of sight, Jerrica touched one of her earrings and whispered, "Show time, Synergy."

Instantly the computer created a holographic disguise. Jerrica became Jem.

"OK!" she shouted, rushing past the other girls. "Let's go out there and do it!"

Glittering and gorgeous, the Holograms rushed onstage, singing:

This world is one world, babe,
    And we all know it.
Could even be a fun world, babe,
    So let's not blow it!
Up or down,
    Come aroun'—
What's it gonna be?
It's up to you and me, babe!!!

Even before Jem and the Holograms could finish their song, the fans went wild—singing, dancing, shouting, crying. With each new song, they went even wilder. Then there was one long ovation.

But as the Holograms left the stage, a furious Roxy and Stormer were waiting for them. "You pulled a fast one," Roxy screamed. "You found a way of keeping Pizzazz from showing up. Now we'll get all the blame for not going on, while you cop all the glory!"

"You must be out of your minds," cried Kimber. "We don't do stuff like that. That's your kind of thing."

"Look," said Jem. "All we wanted was the best show possible. We haven't tried to get rid of anybody."

"Sure," sneered Roxy. "You were jealous of us."

Suddenly Shana pointed. "There she is!"

Pizzazz was running toward them.

"Go after Raymond and Zipper!" she shouted breathlessly at the Holograms as she came up. "They took all the ticket money and locked me up. I just got away. They already have a big head start. It may be too late. But I heard them say they're going out to a farm off River Road. They have a helicopter!"

"Come on!" cried Jem. And the Holograms raced away to the Rockin' Roadster, leaving the Misfits to go onstage.
"Does anybody know where River Road is?" asked Jem.
"I do," said Rio. "But where's Jerrica?"
"No time to tell her," said Jem. "Let's just go."
And they sped off.

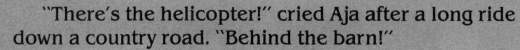

"There's the helicopter!" cried Aja after a long ride down a country road. "Behind the barn!"

"Hold on!" said Jem as she drove onto the field.

"Will you finally get this thing started!" they heard Raymond shrieking at Zipper.

"OK, I fixed it, boss. You can get in now."

"Not a chance!" yelled Rio. Everyone swarmed out of the car, surrounding Raymond and all the money.

After dropping off Raymond and Zipper at the nearest police station, the Holograms and Rio hurried back to the stadium. The Misfits had just ended the concert, and word of the theft was spreading.

"Look!" yelled one of the reporters. "I think they got back the money!"

All the reporters mobbed Jem, Aja, Shana, and Kimber. But they couldn't hear them for an hour…because the fans just would simply not stop cheering.

"Well, everybody," said Rio, dropping in at Starlight Mansion the next day with a batch of newspapers in his arms. "It's headline time!"

"Oh, show us!" said the girls.

He looked around. "I'll wait for Jem," he said.

"She's sleeping," said Jerrica with a little smile. "We'll show her later."

"OK, here it is," said Rio. And he held up a paper in front of them.